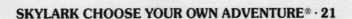

SKYLARK CHOOSE YOUR OWN ADVENTURE® · 21

"I DON'T LIKE CHOOSE YOUR OWN ADVENTURE® BOOKS. I LOVE THEM!" says Jessica Gordon, age ten. And now kids between the ages of six and nine can choose their own adventure too. Here's what kids have to say about the Skylark Choose Your Own Adventure® books.

"These are my favorite books because you can pick whatever choice you want—and the story is all about you."
—**Katy Alson,** *age 8*

"I love finding out how my story will end."
—**Joss Williams,** *age 9*

"I like all the illustrations!"
—**Savitri Brightfield,** *age 7*

"A six-year-old friend and I have lots of fun making the decisions together."
—**Peggy Marcus** *(adult)*

Bantam Skylark Books in the Choose Your Own
  Adventure® Series
Ask your bookseller for the books you have missed

#1 THE CIRCUS

#2 THE HAUNTED HOUSE

#3 SUNKEN TREASURE

#4 YOUR VERY OWN ROBOT

#5 GORGA, THE SPACE MONSTER

#6 THE GREEN SLIME

#7 HELP! YOU'RE SHRINKING

#8 INDIAN TRAIL

#9 DREAM TRIPS

#10 THE GENIE IN THE BOTTLE

#11 THE BIGFOOT MYSTERY

#12 THE CREATURE FROM MILLER'S POND

#13 JUNGLE SAFARI

#14 THE SEARCH FOR CHAMP

#15 THE THREE WISHES

#16 DRAGONS!

#17 WILD HORSE COUNTRY

#18 SUMMER CAMP

#19 THE TOWER OF LONDON

#20 TROUBLE IN SPACE

#21 MONA IS MISSING

MONA IS MISSING

SHANNON GILLIGAN

ILLUSTRATED BY LESLIE MORRILL

An R.A. Montgomery Book

A BANTAM SKYLARK BOOK®
TORONTO · NEW YORK · LONDON · SYDNEY · AUCKLAND

RL 3, 007–009

MONA IS MISSING

A Bantam Skylark Book / October 1984

CHOOSE YOUR OWN ADVENTURE® is a registered
trademark of Bantam Books, Inc.

Original conception of Edward Packard.

Skylark Books is a registered trademark of Bantam Books, Inc.
Registered in U.S. Patent and Trademark Office and elsewhere.

Front cover art by Ralph Reese.

ISBN 0-553-15283-1

Published simultaneously in the United States and Canada

PRINTED IN THE UNITED STATES OF AMERICA

CW   0 9 8 7 6 5 4 3 2 1

For my parents

READ THIS FIRST!!!

Most books are about other people.

This book is about you—and your camel, Mona.

What happens to you depends on what you decide to do.

Do not read this book from the first page through to the last page. Instead, start on page one and read until you come to your first choice. Then turn to the page shown and see what happens.

When you come to the end of a story, go back and start again. Every choice leads to a new adventure.

Good luck!

It is early morning in Abu Diyab, the village **1** in Egypt where you live. No one else is up, but you are wide awake. You feel that something is wrong. When you walk downstairs and out the back door, you know what it is. The courtyard is empty. Mona, your camel, is missing!

Mona has escaped three times before. Each time she has gotten into a lot of trouble. Your parents said that if it ever happened again, they would have to sell Mona.

You run out of the courtyard and quickly look around. In one direction, you can see all the way down to the Nile River. In the other direction are the rocky cliffs that separate your village's green farmlands from the desert. You can't see Mona anywhere.

Turn to page 2.

2   Even though Mona is still small, she is strong and fast. It is very hard to catch her alone. But you don't have much time. Your parents will be awake any minute.

Maybe Mona is at the lemon groves on the edge of town. Mona *loves* lemons.

Should you go straight to the lemon groves by yourself? Or should you get your cousin Ali to help you search?

If you decide to go to the lemon groves by yourself, turn to page 7.

If you decide to get your cousin, turn to page 8.

4   You and Ali get ready to chase the nomads. First you fill small leather pouches with water. You don't know how far you'll have to go, and the desert is hot and dry. Without water, you could die in a few hours.

Outside the village, Ali spots the wide path of camel tracks leading into the desert. You follow the tracks until your village is far behind. When you finally stop to rest, the sun is high overhead. You are very hot. There are still no nomads in sight.

Turn to page 10.

You run across the fields to the lemon **7** groves. It looks as if Mona has been here. Half-eaten lemons are all around, and camel tracks are everywhere.

You search the tracks carefully for clues. They lead out of the grove in two different directions. One set of tracks leads toward the rocky cliffs and the desert beyond. The other tracks lead down to the Nile.

Which set of tracks is Mona's? Or are they both hers? You look at the tracks again. It is impossible to tell.

If you decide to follow the tracks down to the Nile, turn to page 11.

If you decide to follow the tracks toward the desert, turn to page 20.

8   You dash through the narrow winding streets of your village on your way to Ali's house. Ali is an early riser. You find him alone in his yard, washing at the well.

"Ali!" you cry. "I need your help. Mona has escaped again. We have to find her before my parents find out, or I'm afraid they'll sell her."

"Where do you think she's gone?" Ali asks, quickly drying his hands on his long striped robe.

"She probably went to the lemon groves. Mona loves lemons, and she's gone there before when—"

Before you can finish, Ali snaps his fingers and yells, "I know where she is!"

Turn to page 16.

10   "Our water is half-gone," Ali says. "We shouldn't go much farther. I'm sorry. I thought it would be easier to catch the nomads."

Your eyes rest on the tracks leading over the next sand dune. You hate to give up on Mona. But, after all, you aren't even sure the nomads have her.

If you decide Ali is right and you want to turn back right away, turn to page 13.

If you decide to go just a little bit farther before returning to the village, turn to page 14.

You follow the tracks toward the Nile. They lead to the top of a hill looking down to the water. Then the tracks get lost in the rocky soil. Where can Mona be?

Once again you stare at the horizon and all the fields along the river bank. The Nile looks different. Then it hits you in a flash. The water is rising.

The floods have come!

Turn to page 21.

As you walk back to the village, the sun **13** burns hotter than ever. Your mouth feels sticky and dry. Two miles from the village, you and Ali drink your last drop of water.

There is nothing to do but keep walking. Neither of you says much. Then Ali cries, "Look!"

You can't believe what you see. In the distance is a garden filled with flowers and trees. And in the center of the garden is a beautiful painted palace.

Turn to page 17.

14   "Let's go a little farther, Ali," you plead. "Just to the top of the next sand dune."

Ali agrees and follows after you.

You're in luck! The nomads have stopped to pitch camp at the bottom of the next hill.

You glance over the pack of camels and spot Mona at once. The nomads usually guard their animals. But no one seems to be nearby.

"Ali, now is our chance," you whisper. "No one is looking. Let's grab Mona and ride her home as fast as we can."

"But someone might see us! Then what happens?" Ali asks. "I think we should wait and take Mona after dark. If there's a guard, he's bound to fall asleep sometime."

If you decide to steal Mona now while everyone is busy pitching tents, turn to page 24.

If you decide on Ali's plan and wait until dark to escape with Mona, turn to page 32.

16 Ali continues, "Remember the caravan of nomads, the desert wanderers who stopped in town this week? They've stolen camels before if they needed them. I bet *they* took Mona. It makes perfect sense! The same day they leave, Mona is missing!"

"But where are they now?" you ask.

"They're probably crossing the desert. They were supposed to leave today, before sunrise. I think we should go after them and try to bring Mona back."

What Ali says might be true. But on the other hand, you can't believe that Mona was stolen without a fuss.

If you want to chase the nomads with Ali, turn to page 4.

If you want to try the lemon groves first, turn to page 18.

"Come on," you say, "let's go take a look!"

"Wait!" Ali shouts. "Haven't you ever heard of a mirage? When people in the desert run out of water, they sometimes see things that aren't really there. Then they go so far out of their way chasing the mirage that they're lost."

Ali could be right. But the palace *looks* so real.

If you try to persuade Ali to visit the palace, turn to page 43.

If you decide that it's safer to continue back to the village, turn to page 41.

18 On your way to the lemon groves, you and Ali run into Um Tamara, the village gossip.

"You're just the person I wanted to see," Um Tamara cackles, pointing a bony finger at your chest. "Yes, indeed. Early this morning, while it was still dark, I was watching the street from my balcony. Faruk, the camel dealer, suddenly came sneaking around the corner. Who is he leading by the nose? Why, your Mona, of course. Yes, I saw it with my own eyes."

"Faruk? With Mona?" you ask. You can't believe it.

"Yes, yes. It was your Mona, all right," Um Tamara says. "And if I were you, I'd get over to the market before he has a chance to sell her."

If you decide to believe Um Tamara and search for Mona at Faruk's stall, turn to page 26.

If you decide that Um Tamara's story is just gossip, and continue to the lemon groves with Ali, turn to page 27.

20   "Oh, Mona," you say aloud, "please don't go into the desert. The desert is dangerous, even for a camel." As you set off, you promise yourself not to go far. You just hope that Mona hasn't gone far either. That is, if these *are* her tracks.

The sun rises quickly overhead. Carefully you climb the steep path up the rocky cliffs. Now all you see, in every direction for miles and miles, is sand dunes.

Turn to page 22.

Each August, heavy rains in the mountains of Ethiopia and Sudan make the Nile swell. All the farms nearby are flooded. In a bad year, even parts of your village are flooded.

You know that the floods are important to everyone who lives along the Nile. They cover the fields with rich new mud and bring water for crops. But the floods can also be dangerous. Sometimes the water carries people away.

Right now the river is rising fast! Soon it will go crashing over the dikes and rushing into the fields—the fields you have to cross to get home.

If you think you can make it back to the village in time, turn to page 30.

If you think it's too dangerous to cross the fields with the river so high, turn to page 38.

22 For a long time you follow the tracks into the hot desert. The sand is burning under your feet. You are so thirsty that you're beginning to feel dizzy. Just when you're sure you can't go

any farther, you see a small group of trees— **23**
date palms.

You've come to an oasis. What luck!

Turn to page 34.

24   Carefully you and Ali creep into the pack of grazing camels. While Ali stands guard, you try to unravel the knot that ties Mona to the other camels. Mona squeals with delight. She won't stop kissing you hello. It doesn't help.

"Shh, Mona! Quiet," you whisper.

The knot is giving you trouble. Suddenly a voice from behind bellows, "Stop where you are!"

You turn and see an evil-looking man standing over you. In his hand is a long, curved dagger. You look around for Ali. He's gone!

Turn to page 46.

26 You turn and hurry toward the village market. It has just opened. You thread your way past the vegetable and fruit stands, past the seller of sweets. When you reach Faruk's stall, it is completely empty. No Faruk—and no Mona, either.

You ask the cotton seller, dozing nearby, "Where is Faruk? Where are all his camels?"

Turn to page 28.

When you and Ali reach the lemon groves, **27**
Mona is not there. She's not in any of the
nearby fields stealing grain or clover either. You
and Ali look for the nomads next, but you can't
find their tracks. At last you check Faruk's
camel stall in the market. There is no Mona in
sight.

Something is wrong. Whenever Mona escaped before, you always found her in a few
hours. When you go home to tell your parents
at lunch, you find out why.

"Many of the villagers' camels are missing,"
your father tells you. "They think that the
nomads took them. That tribe of nomads is
evil. They're dangerous, too. No one dares go
after them."

Turn to page 49.

28   The cotton seller jolts awake. "Wha—what? Faruk? You want to buy a camel?"

"No," Ali answers. "We don't want to *buy* a camel. We're looking for one, a young camel named Mona. Someone said Faruk had her."

The cotton seller yawns. "Well, if Faruk had your camel, you're out of luck. This morning, he sold every camel he had to the nomads. He got a good price, too."

You and Ali look at each other.

"Come on," Ali cries. "We've got to find those nomads, and quickly!"

The End

30   You run down the hill toward the village as fast as you can. You hope your family is all right!

You round some bushes and *smack*—you run right into Mona! She's running uphill as fast as you're running down. When you look past her, you see why. Mona is running from a three-foot wall of water that is rushing over the fields right behind her.

You leap onto Mona's back, and she gallops back up the path you've just run down. By the time you reach the top of the hill, the fields are covered by the dark, churning water.

You hug your camel in thanks. Not only have you found Mona—she has saved your life!

The End

32   You and Ali wait in the hot sun all afternoon. Now and then you peek over the dune to check on Mona. You see that there's a guard right next to her.

Finally the sun goes down. The desert—so hot in the day—gets very cold.

Several more hours pass. The guard nods off. You can hear his snores all the way to where you and Ali lie in the cold sand. Shivering, you cross to where Mona is tied up. The moon is bright, and you have no trouble finding her among the other camels. Mona seems to sense the danger. Luckily for you, she makes no sound.

When you get Mona's knot untied, you lead her slowly up the dune and out of sight. You and Ali climb onto her back and begin the bumpy gallop home.

Mona is safe!

The End

34   You stumble toward the oasis. You reach the cool pool of water just in time. You've been getting weaker by the minute. This water will save your life!

You fall down on your hands and knees and slurp up the water. After drinking as much as you can, you collapse under the shady palm trees.

Turn to page 45.

Laughing, the woman replies, "Why, I am your Mona, of course."

You and Ali look at each other. Maybe this *is* a mirage!

The beautiful woman says, "I wasn't always a camel. Thousands of years ago, my name was Ismet. I came from a large happy family. We lived in this palace. My sisters and I were famous for our beauty, but my oldest sister, Sesma, was the most beautiful of all. One day the young Pharaoh, king of all Egypt, saw Sesma and fell in love with her. They planned to marry."

"What happened?" Ali asks.

Ismet answers, "There was a goddess who secretly loved the Pharaoh. She was jealous of Sesma. So she put a curse on our whole family. Each of us had to become a work animal for one thousand lives."

Turn to page 50.

38   It is too dangerous to try to cross the fields now. You wait on the hill instead—and it's lucky you do. As you watch, the floodwaters rush over the river bank and cover the fields below.

Within minutes the hill you're on has become an island surrounded by muddy red water. There is nothing to do but sit and wait until a boat is sent to rescue you.

You stare off, feeling very sad. Unless Mona was on high ground, she is probably lost forever.

The End

40   You run out into the yard. Mona is busily chomping on grass. Your father is bent down, checking her legs.

"Is she all right, Father?" you ask.

"Yes. She has a bad cut on her left front leg. And as you can see, she's very hungry. But she will be fine."

Turn to page 48.

At noon you and Ali reach the first well outside the village. You both drink until you're full.

"I guess I have to tell my parents about Mona," you say. "Besides, I've been gone all morning. They'll be wondering where I am."

"All right," Ali agrees. "So we'll meet later and keep searching?"

You nod and smack your palm against Ali's in the Egyptian sign of friendship.

On the way home, you wonder how you're going to explain everything. But when you walk into your courtyard, who is standing there munching clover but Mona!

"Mother! Mother!" you call. "Mona is back!"

Your mother sticks her head out the window. "I know. Your father found her in the lentil fields early this morning. Where have you been? You're late for lunch."

You roll your eyes and laugh. Wait till Ali hears about this!

The End

"But Ali," you plead, "the palace *must* be **43** real. If it were a mirage, we wouldn't *both* see it."

Ali stops. Slowly he smiles. "You're right," he says. "Let's go."

Up close, the garden is even more beautiful than you thought. Rare flowers and fruits grow everywhere. You and Ali drink your fill from a fountain of cool, sparkling water.

A voice from the palace steps calls out, "Welcome. You have searched hard and well to find me. I am glad."

You turn to see a tall beautiful woman dressed in a white shift. She wears a heavy gold collar and bracelets studded with jewels. Even her sandals are gold.

You blurt out, "Who are you?"

Turn to page 37.

Something nuzzles your face. What is it? **45**
You look up.

It's Mona!

You've never been so glad to see anyone in your life. Mona is happy, too. She gives you big wet kisses.

The sun is low in the sky. You must have slept. In an hour the desert will be cool enough for you to return to the village. Only this time you'll get a fast, swooping ride on Mona's back.

The End

46 "Come with me!" the man with the dagger snaps, grabbing your arm. He takes you to the chief's tent and explains how he found you.

The chief is eating. He smacks his lips and says, "Normally, we put camel thieves to death. But you are lucky. One of my wives needs a new servant, so your life will be spared."

You spend the rest of the day fanning the chief's wife. At every thought of your village, you blink back the tears. Your only hope is that Ali will somehow save you.

The End

48   You hug Mona tightly around the neck, rubbing your face against her curly fur. Mona seems to smile.

"Where were you, Mona? How did you come back? Did you escape from the nomads?"

"Yunn, yunn," Mona answers.

Your father laughs and pats Mona on the back. "Well, Mona, a camel as loyal as you, we will always forgive."

"And we will never sell," your mother adds, winking.

The End

You're glad that you didn't hunt for the nomads after all. But it doesn't make you feel any better about Mona.

The next few days are awful. Life is not the same without Mona to feed and ride and play with. You cry yourself to sleep three nights in a row. On the fourth morning, it's still dark when someone shakes you awake.

"Wake, my child," says your mother. "Mona is back. She has returned!"

"What?" you ask, still half-asleep. Is this a dream?

Turn to page 40.

"Couldn't the Pharaoh do anything?" you ask.

"Well, he tried," Ismet says with a sigh. "He convinced the goddess to let my family be together as we were for one day every year. Today was that day, but now it is over. I must return to my other life."

As Ismet finishes talking, the wind begins to blow. Sand starts to sting your skin. You and Ali crouch down and cover your eyes.

Two or three minutes pass. Then the wind dies down as suddenly as it arose.

You open your eyes. The palace has disappeared. The fountain and gardens are gone too. But most amazing of all, Mona stands in front of you, waiting patiently to carry you and Ali back home.

The End

ABOUT THE AUTHOR

Shannon Gilligan graduated from Williams College in 1981. While a student, she spent a year studying at Doshisha University in Kyoto, Japan. When she's not traveling to do research for her books, she lives in Warren, Vermont.

ABOUT THE ILLUSTRATOR

Leslie Morrill is a designer and illustrator whose work has won him numerous awards. He has illustrated over thirty books for children, including the Bantam Classic edition of *The Wind in the Willows; Indian Trail,* a Bantam Skylark Choose Your Own Adventure® book; and *Lost on the Amazon* and *Mountain Survival,* both Choose Your Own Adventure® books. His work has also appeared frequently in *Cricket* magazine. A graduate of the Boston Museum School of Fine Arts, Mr. Morrill lives near Boston, Massachusetts.

Now you can have your favorite Choose Your Own Adventure® Series in a variety of sizes. Along with the popular pocket size, Bantam has introduced the Choose Your Own Adventure® series in a Skylark edition and also in Hardcover.

Now not only do you get to decide on how you want your adventures to end, you also get to decide on what size you'd like to collect them in.

SKYLARK EDITIONS

☐	15238	The Circus #1 E. Packard	$1.95
☐	15207	The Haunted House #2 R. A. Montgomery	$1.95
☐	15208	Sunken Treasure #3 E. Packard	$1.95
☐	15233	Your Very Own Robot #4 R. A. Montgomery	$1.95
☐	15308	Gorga, The Space Monster #5 E. Packard	$1.95
☐	15309	The Green Slime #6 S. Saunders	$1.95
☐	15195	Help! You're Shrinking #5 E. Packard	$1.95
☐	15201	Indian Trail #8 R. A. Montgomery	$1.95
☐	15191	The Genie In the Bottle #10 J. Razzi	$1.95
☐	15222	The Big Foot Mystery #11 L. Sonberg	$1.95
☐	15223	The Creature From Millers Pond #12 S. Saunders	$1.95
☐	15226	Jungle Safari #13 E. Packard	$1.95
☐	15227	The Search For Champ #14 S. Gilligan	$1.95
☐	15241	Three Wishes #15 S. Gilligan	$1.95
☐	15242	Dragons! #16 J. Razzi	$1.95
☐	15261	Wild Horse Country #17 L. Sonberg	$1.95
☐	15262	Summer Camp #18 J. Gitenstein	$1.95
☐	15270	The Tower of London #19 S. Saunders	$1.95
☐	15271	Trouble In Space #20 J. Woodcock	$1.95

<u>Prices and availability subject to change without notice.</u>

Buy them at your local bookstore or use this handy coupon for ordering:

**Bantam Books, Inc., Dept. AVSK, 414 East Golf Road,
Des Plaines, Ill. 60016**

Please send me the books I have checked above. I am enclosing
$_____ (please add $1.25 to cover postage and handling). Send
check or money order—no cash or C.O.D.'s please.

Mr/Ms _____

Address _____

City/State _____ Zip _____

AVSK—9/84
Please allow four to six weeks for delivery. This offer expires 3/85.

SPECIAL
MONEY SAVING
OFFER

Now you can have an up-to-date listing of Bantam's hundreds of titles plus take advantage of our unique and exciting bonus book offer. A special offer which gives you the opportunity to purchase a Bantam book for only 50¢. Here's how!

By ordering any five books at the regular price per order, you can also choose any other single book listed (up to a $4.95 value) for just 50¢. Some restrictions do apply, but for further details why not send for Bantam's listing of titles today!

Just send us your name and address plus 50¢ to defray the postage and handling costs.